D0460636
This book belongs to
Eliasand pavia

A Read-Aloud Storybook

Adapted by Ellen Titlebaum

Visit www.disneybooks.com, a part of the GO Network

 For information address Mouse Works, 114 Fifth Avenue, New York, New York 10011-5690.
Printed in the United States of America.
Based on the Pooh stories by A. A. Milne (copyright The Pooh Properties Trust).
ISBN 0-7364-1002-3

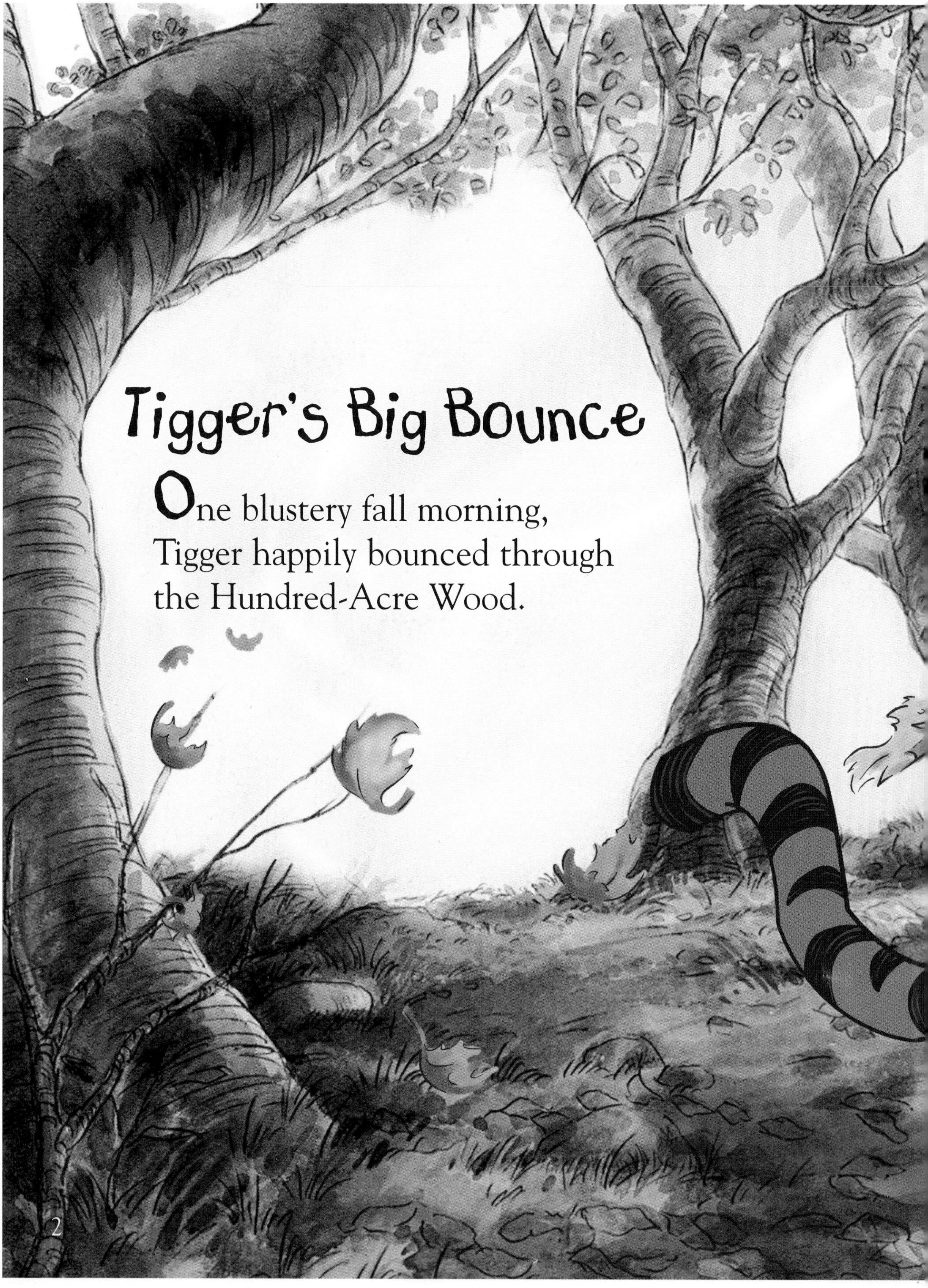

Tigger's Big Bounce

One blustery fall morning, Tigger happily bounced through the Hundred-Acre Wood.

Soon Tigger bounced right into Winnie the Pooh. "Wanna go bouncin' with me?" asked Tigger.

"I *would* go bouncing with you," replied Pooh, "except that I have to count my honeypots to make sure I have enough for winter."

Next Tigger bounced into Piglet.

But Piglet could not bounce with Tigger either. He was busy collecting firewood. And Kanga was busy sweeping.

So Tigger bounced all by himself until he BOUNCE-BOUNCE-BOUNCED onto a branch . . . which pushed over a great big rock . . . which rolled down a hill . . .

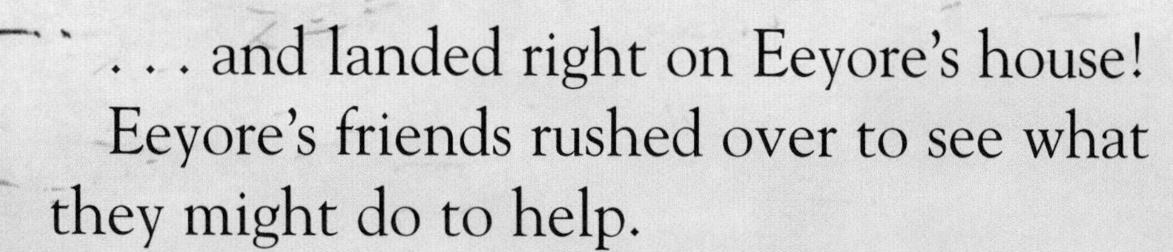

. . . and landed right on Eeyore's house!
Eeyore's friends rushed over to see what they might do to help.

"Your attention, please," said Rabbit. "I have officially completed the plans." Rabbit organized an enormous rock-moving machine. But the boulder wouldn't budge.

Finally, Tigger bounced up. He could see that a big bounce would get Rabbit's rock-moving machine going.

But Tigger's bounce made the machine get going too quickly!

"You ruin everything with your bouncing!" said Rabbit.

"But that's what tiggers do best," said Tigger.

"What we're trying to say," said Piglet, "is that we can't bounce like tiggers because . . ."

". . . we're not tiggers," finished Pooh sadly.

Roo followed Tigger as he walked off. Suddenly Tigger brightened. "Say—if there are other tiggers, we could all bounce morning, noon, and nighty-night, too!"

The Family Tree

Tigger and Roo went to Owl to find out how to find other tiggers. Owl explained, "To find one's family, one must find one's family tree."

"Say, thanks for the tip, Beak-Lips!" cried Tigger as he and Roo bounced off.

Arriving with a great big bounce, Tigger asked his friends if they had seen any members of the tigger family tree. But no one had.

“I didn’t know Tigger had a family,” said Piglet.
“Seemed to be looking for ’em,” added Eeyore.
“We must be supposed to help them,” said Pooh. “I often remember to forget these sorts of things.”

But, after a long search, Tigger and Roo returned home without having found a single other tigger.

"If there were other tiggers, we could all bounce the Whoop-de-Dooper Loop-de-Looper Alley-Ooper Bounce," said Tigger sadly.

Wanting to be just like Tigger, Roo tried the bounce, too. *Crash!* He landed in an open closet—where he found a locket.

"It must have a picture of my tigger family inside!" cried Tigger. But the locket was empty.

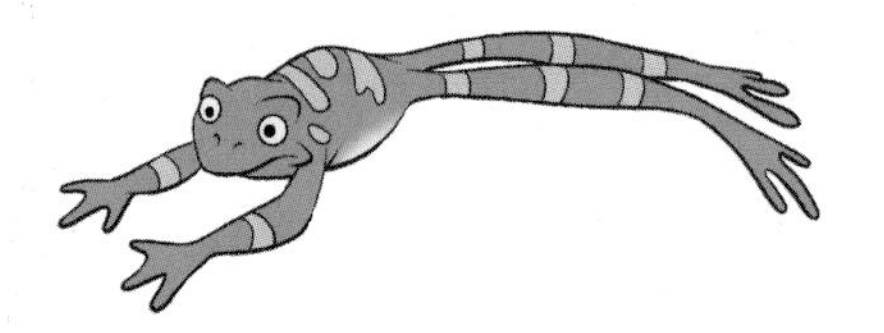

Meanwhile, Eeyore announced, "I found 'em—Tigger's family." He led Pooh and Piglet to a pond full of striped, bouncy frogs. Could this be Tigger's family?

"Tigger misses you very much," said Pooh to a frog. But the frog just hopped away.

Then, in a nearby tree, Pooh found some bees—*striped* bees. Bees that looked just a little bit like Tigger.

"Oh, bother!" Pooh said when the bees started to chase him and Piglet and Eeyore. "I don't think these bees are the right sorts of tiggers."

Poor Tigger was no closer to finding his family.

"Why don't you write them a letter?" suggested Roo.

"Hoo-hoo-*hoo!*" hooted Tigger happily. And he began to write.

Tiggr

Tigger mailed his letter and waited for a response. But none came. Roo grew worried about his friend.

Kanga said, "As long as we care for him, he always will be one of our family."

A Letter for Tigger

The next day, Roo gathered everyone except Tigger at Owl's house. Roo wanted Owl to write a letter to Tigger from his family.

Owl began the letter: "Dear Tigger, Just a note to say . . ."

“Dress warmly,” suggested Kanga.
“Eat well,” added Pooh.
“Stay safe and sound,” said Piglet.
“Keep smilin’,” rumbled Eeyore.
“We’re always there for you,” said Roo.
Owl finished the letter: “Wishing you all the best, Signed, Your Family.”

The next morning, Tigger showed off the letter from his family. "They're comin' ta see me, TOMORROW!"

"Where does it say that?" asked Owl, surprised.

"Nowhere!" said Tigger. "'Cause with us tiggers ya gotta read betwixt the lines."

Now Roo had a new idea: the friends would pretend to be Tigger's long-lost family! Everyone painted on stripes and practiced their bouncing.

That evening, Tigger welcomed his family. "Let's all do what tiggers do best! That's bouncin', of course."

Roo tried to bounce the Whoop-de-Dooper Loop-de-Looper Alley-Ooper Bounce but crashed into the closet . . . again.

Roo's mask fell off. Then Tigger pulled off the others' masks as well.

Tigger was so disappointed. "There's a tigger family tree fulla my REAL family, and I'm gonna find 'em!" he said, and left.

Rabbit, Pooh, Piglet, Eeyore, and Roo followed after Tigger. "Tigger! Tigger!" they called into the raging snow.

Deep in the forest, Tigger had just found a tree so grand and gleaming that it had to be the tigger family tree!

"Whoohoohoo!" called Tigger. But no one was home. Tigger sadly dropped his letter.

Tigger's letter soared off into the wind, and landed right in Roo's hand. He started running toward the giant tree, with the others right behind him.

"What are you guyses doing here?" Tigger asked.

"We came all this way to look for you!" explained Rabbit.

Tigger began to argue that he was waiting for his tigger family when a low rumble echoed through the valley.

Suddenly an avalanche was coming right at them! Tigger bounced everyone to safety in his tree. But the snow rolled Tigger toward a steep cliff!

Doing a perfect Whoop-de-Dooper Loop-de-Looper Alley-Ooper Bounce, Roo rescued Tigger.

Taking a long look at little Roo
and his other good friends, Tigger knew
his family had been with him all along.

The next day Tigger gave a party for all his friends. As a special treat, he gave Roo his heart-shaped locket.

"Now wait half a minute!" Tigger cried excitedly. "We need to take a family portrait to put in it."

And that's exactly what they did.